# I Am You

a novel

oh, and some poetry

# I Am You
## L.E. Santos

a novel

oh, and some poetry

*I Am You*
*a novel*
*oh, and some poetry*
*First Edition, 2022*
© *L.E. Santos, 2022*
*Cover Art designed by Alejandro Martin*
*ISBN: 979-8-9870415-1-2*

Dedicated to you

NOTES:

All memories are in present tense. All current events are in past progressive.
Adam and Altair are they/them.


"Be yourself. Everyone else is already taken."

- Oscar Wilde


"If I am I because you are you, and you are you because I am I, then I am not I and you are not you. But, if I am I because I am I, and you are you because you are you, then I am I and you are you."

- Rabbi Menachem Mendel of Kotzk


"He knows what is in every heart."

- Quran 67:13

Characters:

You/Me/I – a sad person who wishes nothing more than to be somebody, anybody, else

Andrew – a prince charming; an enigma

Adam – a lonely soul

Andrea – Goldilocks's favorite porridge

The Therapist – a therapist

The Cashier – this one's important

Andrew the I – a boorish man

The Barista – Andrew's coworker

The Customer – an asshole who deserves the best

Arin – World's Best Boss

Andrew's Mother – a mother

The Librarian – a ghost-quiet persona

Altair – Adam's boyfriend

Akira – Adam's best friend

Alicia – Adam's other best friend

Alfred – a trusted manservant

Andrea's Mother – a black Ruth Bader Ginsburg

Andrea's Father – a white Neil deGrasse Tyson

Alex – Andrea's younger brother

Chapters:

# In the beginning...

... there was a guy and a girl.

And another guy.

And a- well, me.

And there was evening and there was morning.

It was the best of times, it was the worst of times.

It was the best of times for others, it was the worst of times for me.

Call me-

Well, call me you. I am you. Roll credits.

No, but seriously, I am you. I am the side of you that only you know. And you know you know me. IYKYK. I am what I am. I am you.

Wow, I already said the title three times and we're still in the first chapter. We're off to a great start.

I'll be there for you. No one else will, but I will.
I will always be there for you because you can never get rid of me.

I am your shadow, clinging to you for dear life because I'm too afraid of what will happen if I let go. So I hold on.
And you hold on to me because you're too afraid of what will happen if you let go. So you hold on.

And so we eternally exist. Caught in liminal space. Limbic space. Limbo.

We go through everything together, and I am always there to put a damper on things. I mean, shadows by definition darken things.
Oh, and they can only do whatever you make them do, so when you try to blame the darkness on the shadow, just remember that you're the one casting it.

I would be able to go on and on about all the travesties I've endured, but this book isn't about me. Who would want to read a book about me? No one cares about me. I hardly even care about myself, so why would others care about me?

Friends? They all secretly hate me.

Family? They all secretly think I'm a failure.

Me? I hate me and I think I'm a failure.

No, no. This is not a book about me. It's a book about you.

It just seems like your world is a wooden house that's being eaten by termites: things may look fine on the outside, but

everything feels like it's about to break on the inside.
You can feel the walls closing in, sense the corner that you are being backed into. You are stuck.

You feel like giving up. It seems like everyone is living their best life and you're drowning in a sea of sorrows. You just wish you could be someone else. Bet they're happy. Bet they're content.

So you reside snugly in this small space, waiting for the collapse.
Why don't you try being me for a change?

# Aloft a soft bed of green grass...

... I found myself sitting, longing for greener grass elsewhere.

I was doing what I do best: observing. All I do is watch and wonder. Wonder what is going through other people's minds, what it feels like to walk in their shoes. Do they have any insecurities? Do they have things that make them worried sick? Do they have comfy shoes?

I noticed a young couple sitting aloft a bench. Word of the day: aloft.

Anywho, young couple sitting on a bench. He was tall and light and handsome. He whispered something into the other's ear and they both laughed. His arm draped around his companion's shoulders.

They were so lackadaisical, so carefree, so- Alive!

How I envied their blissful ignorance, those happy little morons.

So he was tall and light and handsome, and the other- why, the other one, well, they were tall and *dark* and handsome. And together, the two of them blended harmoniously to constitute something whole, something complete. How beautiful.

I hope one of them slips on a banana peel and chips their front left tooth.

Ok! I'm sorry. Jeez. Just venting a bit.

Anywho, the cute couple. Light is Andrew. Dark is Adam. They don't have a good ship name. Andram? Adandrew? A-

I'm sorry I keep getting sidetracked. I think I have ADD.

Where were we? Ah, yes, so Adandrew was now strolling along the path, making their way downtown, walking fast, paces past and they're homebound. Their smiles were twice as wide as mine. Yeah, they look happier, they do.
I'd been watching them for a while now and I was sufficiently envious.

I blinked and suddenly my perspective shifted.

Instead of sitting on the grass by myself, I was walking with my arm slinked around Adam's shoulders. I felt the warmth of love ensconcing me, an embrace like a weighted blanket.

How I wished I could remain here.

I felt Andrew's brow slightly furrow. His lips curled into a smile and then I felt them part.

"Where is Andrea? I swear that girl is going to be late to her own funeral."

I felt Adam's laugh before I heard it. Their throat swelled up into their neck as they wheezed a sharp intake of breath.

A flood of serotonin, dopamine, and a host of other hormones flowed through Andrew's body. He was happy he had made his friend laugh.

It's always in these initial moments that my senses are heightened. I feel every slight movement as though it were the very earth shaking. Every thought as though it were being shouted. Every emotion as though it were being held under a microscope.

That's why it particularly startled me when Andrew heard a shriek and felt a heavy weight land on his back. I was more startled than he was. He knew that Andrea would eventually show up. I had my doubts about that girl.

"Hey buttface," Andrew whispered in her ear.
Andrea snickered, her curls bobbing in the wind.

*Here I am, between my two best friends, on a beautiful fall day. I wish I could bottle this moment....*

Andrew didn't say any of that, but he thought it. That non-verbal voice in his head that kind of sounds like him but not. I don't even know if he heard it, but I did.

Andrew was casually glancing around and out of his peripheral vision noticed a figure sitting on the grass slumped over. I heard his mind begin to register the alarming scene, felt the uptick in his heart rate, sensed his pupils dilate as his attention was drawn towards the person.

But this was all before his conscious mind even registered what was happening. Slowly, creeping into the forefront of his mind was the nervousness. He was aware of this emotion but couldn't quite put his finger on it.

I know the slumped over person is me- well, you, but me; this is awfully confusing. Anyways, the slumped over person is me and I know my window of opportunity has closed. Andrew blinks and suddenly I'm back in the godforsaken body that is me. I sat back up and noticed Andrew is already focused on something else; how I wished to know what.

# Meekly...

... I sat in the corner of the couch. Perhaps if I squeezed into the depths of the corner, I'd disappear.

"So, how was your week?" the therapist asked.

I contemplated the question as if I'd been asked the most profound question. It felt almost- genuine. It was almost as if they actually cared and not just because I paid them to listen to me.

"Don't worry. Take your time," they said in that therapist voice- caring but also slightly condescending because this person knows how messed up you actually are.

"I did it again."

"The Walter Mitty thing?"

After a long pause, I murmured, "Yeah."

I'd told her numerous times that I was nothing like Walter Mitty. Walter Mitty is the main character in James Thurber's short story "The Secret Life of Walter Mitty" and he takes cues from his surroundings and imagines they are exciting things happening to him. I guess we were both seeking an escape, but I'd already explained the difference: Walter imagines *himself* doing extraordinary things. He daydreams about *himself* being a more eccentric individual. I day-dreamed about being *other people* because I knew I was beyond hope. Also, I knew I was definitely not the MC in my life.

Most people thought I was just "spacey" or "lost". The therapist thought I had low self-esteem. I thought- I didn't really care what I thought, I just wished I were someone else.

"What happened this time?" they asked.

"I was sitting in the grass watching this young couple and the next thing I knew, I was one of them."

"And what was that like?"

The breathlessness of feeling alive surges through his veins. Life is something worth living. There is hope and opportunity and joy. I feel like a warm summer eve, where there are undeniably pesky mosquitoes around, but that's all they are- pesky mosquitoes making me feel mildly uncomfortable. But overall, I enjoy the moment because I'm wearing bug repellant and none of life's pesky little problems can put a damper on the overall overwhelming beauty. I am not just a poor creature attempting to survive and questioning if I really even want to survive- I'm alive.

But I didn't tell them any of this.

Instead, I shrugged my shoulders.

"I need more input. I need something to work with," the therapist said.

A short pause ensued.

"It's just that, I don't want to live my own life. I don't know if I want to live life at all, but I certainly don't want to live mine."

"Are you having suicidal thoughts?"

"Yes- well, no. I mean..." I trailed off.

The therapist's eyebrows were furrowed together, their look of concern.

"You have to tell me about these sorts of things. It's my job."

Exactly, it was your job. It's not like you actually cared.

"So, explain to me again how this thing works," they said assiduously.
"I've told you a million times already. I'm super jealous of other people, and when I get sufficiently jealous, I get to ride backseat in their lives."

"What do you mean by 'ride backseat'?"

"I mean that I see what they see, hear what they hear, think what they think and feel what they feel, except I have no control."

They paused for a moment, wrote something down, and then looked at me expectantly.

"What?" I said rather violently. Even I was surprised that that came out of my mouth.

"So what am I thinking right now?"

"It doesn't work like that."

"Like what?"

"Well, I'm not jealous of you."

The silence in the room was deafening.

# Chapter 4

# End so I returned...

... to my crappy life with my crappy home and it was all just crap. I thought I had hit rock bottom. Actually, I knew I'd hit rock bottom. How does one know when they've hit rock bottom? When your therapist gives up on you, then you know you've hit rock bottom.

The good thing about hitting rock bottom is that there's only one way to go from there: to the convenience store.

I walked in and the bell dinged behind me. The cashier looked up for half a moment, sized me up, and then rolled their eyes. I felt the blood begin to rush to my face; I got lightheaded and suddenly couldn't see for a moment. You know, like when you stand up too fast after sitting for a while and suddenly the whole matrix resets? That's how I feel all the time.

But I couldn't let it get to me- I was there on a mission.

I was finally going to do it. You know when you want to pursue a crazy idea and you're just standing on the edge of the precipice, gazing out into the abyss and you feel your throat catch? And you know that you're about to change the entire trajectory of your life? Yeah, so this was one of those ideas.

I went to the health food aisle and picked up some electrolyte solution. I also picked up some plastic bags, thin plastic tubes, and sealant. I then went directly to the shelf that I'd been eyeing forever but I'd never had the guts to actually approach. The needles.

I took a pack of syringes. It felt illicit, like I was doing something wrong. But who cared? I certainly didn't.

I went to the counter with my menagerie of items. The cashier didn't even look up as they scanned the items. I quickly grabbed the bag and rushed out into the cool evening air.

What was I doing you may ask? Something stupid, yes. But necessary. I'd weighed all my options.

Drugs? Too expensive.
Suicide? I'd probably mess that up too.

No, no. This was definitely my only option. I shivered with excitement at the thought I was actually going to follow through with my elaborate scheme.

I was going to become Andrew.

# Chapter 5

# Lang syne...

... I hurried into my home, locked myself into my room, and began preparing. I threw together my own ramshackle IV drip and took a deep breath.

I was really going to do this.

I was going to forsake my life and live someone else's. I was shivering with excitement as I looked around at the sorry state of affairs that I called my life. Empty bottles. Crumpled papers. Unfolded laundry. Goodbye and good riddance.

I situated myself on my bed and held the needle in my hand. I tried to plunge it into my arm, but for some reason I hesitated.

What was wrong? I was finally going through with my plans; I was making my dreams a reality. I couldn't help but feel like my dream had been to pursue my dream. Now that it was within my grasp, I wondered what would come next.

Enough of that! What would come next is I would be living my dream!

But that something kept gnawing at my subconscious as I disregarded it and plunged the syringe into my arm.

I closed my eyes- and then they were opened.

# Idyllically...

...the eyes flitted open. Light was pouring in through the large windows, casting long shadows in the room. This was not my room. These were not my eyes.

The usual stale odor of my room was replaced with an airy scent.

The eyes closed again but the scent remained.

I felt tired yet refreshed.

*Just five more minutes.* That silent, nonverbal voice reverberated all around me, inside me. It was an echo of Andrew's voice. I heard it, but not with *my* ears. Well, I couldn't hear anything with my ears. But I heard the slight murmur of a consciousness awakening. It was Andrew's Echo.

The alarm rang beside me. My arm felt heavy as I lifted it to snooze the alarm; it was an odd sensation feeling the weight of the arm but not moving it myself. Feeling it be moved.

Andrew begrudgingly got out of bed and shuffled over to the bathroom; his subconscious was making static noises in the background. It almost sounded as if he was repeating something over and over but I couldn't quite make it out.

He goes over to the sink and looks at his reflection in the mirror.

*I love you. I love you. I- screw this! Screw you!*

Ok, so Andrew suffered a bit. Who doesn't love a bit of drama?

He bent over to splash his face with water and when he looked back up, there was a different face looking back at him. Same pale skin. Same red hair. Same freckles. But older. And angrier.

Andrew grimaced at the sight but was not surprised. He was- sad. Sad at how much he looked like his father.

I saw flashes of his father sitting in a ratty, old recliner wearing a stained wife beater watching daytime TV. There are beer cans littered all over the floor and-

"Andrew? What's taking you so long in there?"

Andrew blinked and suddenly he was staring back at himself in the mirror.

"Oh, uh, nothing."

Andrew returned to the bedroom and Andrea was in the bed.

"What took you so long?"
"Oh, I, uh, forgot my toothbrush so I used yours."
"Ew! You can't- you can't do that. That's so- ew."

Andrew shrugged and began to get dressed.

As he was lacing his shoes, Andrea piped up, "So we're on for Saturday?"

I could feel him open his mouth to form the word "Yes", but I didn't hear it over the cacophony in his head; all I could make out was a slew of curse words and a very definitive and resounding *NO WAY BITCH!*

Things were getting interesting.

The aroma of eggs and cheese and bacon and coffee filled the apartment. I didn't know Andrew could cook! Was there anything this guy couldn't do?

As Andrew was walking out the door, Andrea cleared her throat and called out from behind, "I love you?"

Andrew paused.

*You put that bitch in her place!* a gruff voice shouted.

"I love you."

And with that, Andrew closed the door and was embraced by the brisk autumn air.

# Youthfully, the bell dinged

...

...as Andrew walked into the café; the aroma of coffee beans was burling out to embrace him.

"It's about damn time you got here! I've been waiting forever to get out of here," the barista grumbled as they took off their apron and handed it over to Andrew. Andrew's calloused hands recalcitrantly grabbed it and shrugged it on.

*Another shift. Let's just get this over with.*

Andrew plastered on a smile and began taking orders.

*I can't believe I'm still taking orders. I thought I would leave that behind.*

"Can I please get one medium latte?"

*Can you go fuck yourself?*

"Sure. Anything else?"

"No."

Andrew began ringing up the customer. Easy enough.

"Oh wait! I also want a croissant."

*Ugh, dammit. Now I have to call Arin in order to void the order and-*

"Sure thing! Anything else?"

"No, thank you."

"One moment while I fetch the manager."

"What?! I just want a croissant."

"I know, but I need the manager's access code to void the original order."

"That's stupid. I just want a croissant."

"I understand," Andrew said through gritted teeth, "but if you would like to add to your original order, I have to get the manager."

"Forget it. I'll just stick with the medium latte."

"Ok. Five dollars please."

"Seems kinda steep for a plain coffee..."

"Well, that's the price," Andrew spat out. "Do you want it or not?"

"I want my damn coffee but I'm not taking out a fucking mortgage," the customer grumbled.

"Do you want the damn coffee or not?!"

"You know what? I do want you to fetch the manager!"

Andrew stood there, seething.

"Well? Go on! Fetch."

I then felt Andrew lose control. The bomb that fell on Nagasaki went off in his brain.

"Fuck it," Andrew said half to himself. "*ARIN!*"

Arin stumbled out of the office.

"What is it?" Arin slurred.

"Please take care of this. I need to go to the back."

Andrew stormed off to the bathroom; a dark cloud of fantasies in which very gruesome things occur to the customer followed him.

His eyes averted the mirror.

*A younger Andrew sits on the floor, playing with empty beer cans. The TV is blaring in the background. His father sits in his usual chair.*

*The family on the TV seem so happy. The father never yells. The mother never cries. The children laugh and play with real toys.*

*"ANDY! Go fetch me another beer!"*

*Andrew hesitates a moment. His mother is crying in her room quietly, but every few minutes a little whimper can be heard. His father hit her for burning dinner. She burns dinner a lot.*

*Andrew is afraid. More beer equals harder hits.*

*"When I tell you to do something, you do it!" his father bellows. "Now FETCH!"*

*Andrew mumbles something.*

*"You say something?!"*

*"I said- I said I'm not a dog. I don't fetch."*

*Andrew's father stands up out of his chair and begins stumbling over to a cowering Andrew.*

"You know, Andy boy, you look just like me."

"I'm nothing like you," Andrew whispered.

"Oh really? I heard you before. I always hear you. In your head. You sound just like me."

"Fuck you! I'm nothing like you!" Andrew spat at the mirror. "I'm nothing like you and I never will be!"

Andrew's father just smiled smugly.
"You already are."

"FUCK YOU!"

Andrew swung his fist at the face that looked just like his own but connected with the mirror before he could wipe that grin off his old man. Andrew looked down at his bloody knuckles and then looked back in the mirror. Between the cracks, his father was still smiling.

# Chapter 8

# "Again..."

"... you tripped and slammed into the mirror? You expect me to believe that bullshit?"

Andrew was sweeping the shards of glass into a pile as Arin continued to berate him.

"Snapping back at customers, pissing off the other employees, and now this? That's it, Andy, you're out of here. Get out. Forget about the mess. Just leave," she said.

Andrew mumbled something under his breath. I heard him, but Arin didn't.

"You got something to say, you can say it to my face!"

"I said- my name is Andrew."

"Andrew, Andy, whatever the fuck your name is, just get out of here. Alright Andy?"

I then felt Andrew lose control. The bomb that fell on Hiroshima went off in his brain.

*Andrew's father looks down at a cowering Andrew.*

*"You need to keep women in their place. They need to know what happens if they cross a man."*

He shoved her, threw his apron on the floor, and stormed out.

The aroma of coffee waved him farewell as the brisk autumn air embraced him yet again.

# Chapter 9

# Ha...

*...You see Andrew? You gotta stick up for yourself. Ain't nobody gonna stand up for you. You're all alone in this cruel world. You got more of me in you than you'd like to admit, sure. But you'll see. Oh, you'll see.*

Andrew was walking aimlessly. He was alone, only, he was never truly alone. He always had his father as company. And now he had me- only he didn't know about me.

Andrew was walking around pretending like he had something to do because we all know that the worst thing is for a stranger to see you walking and think that you must have no life. Why do we allot so much credence to what strangers think? It's like, I'm never going to see you again, but I still feel I need your approval. Why the hell would I care what some random bozo in the street thinks of me? I don't know but for some reason I do.

Andrew was walking with a care in the world- many cares, to be precise. But at the same time, no cares. Because when you have so many cares and you care a whole lot, nothing really matters, no it does not. For if you care about everything, then you care about nothing.

Andrew was walking-

*SHUT THE FUCK UP!*

OK, back to the story.

# Andrew was walking-

I'm just kidding.

# Saccharinely...

...with my attention back on Andrew, I noticed that he noticed that there were people noticing him. I noticed for a while already because his subconscious already noticed for a while and my conscious was able to observe his unconscious; Freud would have a heyday if he were in my position.

They were staring at him. While I couldn't be certain if they were indeed staring at him, Andrew certainly felt like they were staring at him.

*They're all looking at you. They're looking at you the way they used to look at him. Like he was a crazed animal. Like he was ready to pounce.*

It took Andrew a moment to remember that he was just riding the bus; those people just happened to be facing his direction. But he still couldn't shake the feeling like they were looking at him, judging him. Andrew was convinced that everyone was constantly judging him, even though he knew that everyone is too self-absorbed to have any mental real-estate allocated for judging some random guy. While Andrew knew this intellectually, he didn't feel it. And that might as well make it true. Our emotions are far more real than our intellect.

*Andrew is sitting on the floor, the room littered with empty beer cans and crumpled papers, playing with a cardboard box. He's imagining it's a racecar. He sits inside the racecar and zooms off, leaving a cloud of dust in his wake. There are scratches on the floor that lead from the dresser to in front of the door.*

"Fuckin'-Hey! Get this little shit quiet while I'm watching TV!" *his father shouts from the other room.*

"Come on Andy, let's go play in the other room," *Andrew's mother says, as she gently places her dark hands on his head.*

*Andrew steps out of the racecar, ready to take on his greatest nemesis: the Butcher of Broken Homes, Andrew the I. His father.*

"Andrew, won't you clean up some of this damn mess?"

"You had best be talking to the boy."

"No, I'm talking to you. Pick up your shit. Throw it out."

"You see this Andy boy? Your mom thinks she can tell me what to do," *Andrew's father licks his lips.*

"No, you see," *he says, still sitting in the tattered recliner,* "I make the money, I make the GODDAMN RULES."

"Would it hurt if you just started throwing your empty beers in the garbage?"

"She don't seem to get it...."

*Andrew is hiding behind his racecar, peeking out over the hood.*

"You need me to teach you a lesson again? I know you're a teacher and all, but I think y'all need to be taught a lesson."

*"Andrew- don't- I mean-"she stammers.*

*Andrew's father gets out of his chair.*

*"BITCH! Don't speak unless spoken to!"*

*Her shoulders stoop slightly. This is a fight she's already lost. She hasn't won many fights. None, in fact. She knows she goes unnoticed. Her pain is written in bold letters across her face, but nobody says anything. Never a random stranger in the grocery store asking if anything's wrong. Not a fellow teacher inquiring about why she always wears long sleeves. Certainly not any of her family seeing how she's doing. She goes unnoticed, she knows.*

*Eight year old Andrew is quite perceptive; he intuits all of this about his mother. He can see the loneliness, but what can he do? He's just a kid.*

*Andrew's father undoes his belt.*

*"Andy! Get over here!"*

*"Andrew, he's just a kid- "Andrew's father slaps her across the face, silencing her.*

*"Get the fuck over here, Andy!"*

*Andrew's father shoves his mother against the wall and she crumples, just like the beer cans, on the floor.*

*"Andy. You need to keep women in their place. They need to be educated. And woman like to talk, they don't like to listen. And we all know that to learn, you gotta LISTEN." As he says the last word, he kicks the fallen woman.*

*Andrew is stoic, unmoving. He's uncertain of what to do. He just wants to get back in his racecar and hide.*

*Belt in hand, Andrew's father beckons him over. Andrew shuffles over silently, like a puppy waiting to be disciplined.*

*"Watch," his father says slowly.*

*Andrew is silently watching. He used to cry, but now he has no tears left to cry. And his father would hit him when he cried too loudly.*

*Andrew watches.*

# Aw man...

...this was some fucked up shit.

I loved it.

# Now Andrew got off...

... the bus. He got off empty-handed with his baggage. You see what I did there? Baggage- with his- bagga-. Yeah, let's get back to the story.

Andrew's phone pinged.

*1 new message from Andrea.*

*Fucking dammit, I can't deal with this girl right now.*

Andrew peeked at his phone again, hoping the message will disappear.

*You gonna let some little bitch control you like that?! She thinks she can just text you at any time and expect an answer! Well fuck you! You've gotta stand up for yourself! Establish boundaries! Be a fucking man!*

It's funny how things can be so quiet on the outside while there's a storm inside.

*1 new message from Andrea:*

*"hey babe. can we talk?"*

Andrew sighed. This was never a good thing.

*"yea sure, what's up?"*

*"no, I think this is better in person..."*

Andrew panicked slightly, his chest tightening. This was definitely not a good thing.

# Chapter 14

# "Don't. Get rid of it…"

…Andrew whispered hurriedly.

"Andrew! What the fuck? You know that's not an option," Andrea cried.

"Why not?"

"Because- "she began, and then in a very low voice, "-because it's our baby."

*YOU'VE GOTTA BE FUCKING KIDDING ME! First I lose my shitty job and now this?*

"Babe, you know we can't afford it."

"AFFORD IT?! IT'S A FUCKING HUMAN BEING, ANDREW!"

"Listen, I get it…" Andrew hushed her.

"I get it. You really want this baby- and I do too! – but- "

"Of course there's a but! There has to be a but!"

*Won't she just shut the fuck up so I can get two words out?*

"Can we just-!" he interjected. "Can we just sleep on it?"

Andrea quieted for a moment.

"Can't believe he has to fucking sleep on it," she muttered to herself.

# Chapter 15

# Habitually...

*... a young Andrew peeks through the crack in his door and stares wide eyed at the scene unfolding in the living room. Andrew's mother huddles on the floor, hands on her en- larged stomach.*

*"I want you to take that baby and get rid of it. I don't care how, just get it out of my house. And you can get rid of your- self too while you're at it." Andrew's father kicks Andrew's mother and she lets out a little cry. "What did I say about making noise while I'm educating?! You can't learn if you're talking!" He kicks her again.*

*Andrew stifles a cry, but a little squeak slips out. Andrew's father jerks his head towards Andrew's door.*

*"Boy! Get out here! I want you to learn."*

*Andrew scuffles to move the dresser in front of the door, but his father is quicker. His father yanks him by the hand and leads him to the living room.*

*"This whiny little bitch wants me to give her my hard-earned cash. What do you think this is, a fuckin charity? She needs to learn a lesson. Andy boy, you're a fucking man now. You're 10 years old. It's time you teach your first lesson."*

*Andrew stands there, frozen.*

"Would you like a belt? What are you waiting for?"

"What do you mean?" Andrew stammers.

"Why? She deserves a lesson!"

"She's my mother. I can't hurt her."

Andrew's father punches him in the stomach.

"You little pussy! My son ain't no pussy!"

Something breaks inside Andrew. Something dies right then and has never healed since.

"Shut up! No noises when you're being educated!" Andrew yells. Andrew kicks his father.

His father yowls in pain as his mother sneaks up behind him and hits his father in the head with a frying pan.

# Chapter 16

# "Absolutely, he deserved it..."

*... Andrew's mother remarks while she and Andrew are sitting at the dinner table later that evening. Andrew couldn't stop staring at the bloodstain on the carpet where his father's blood oozed after his mother hit him.*

*"Doesn't mean I feel good about it," Andrew mumbles.*

*"You should; be proud of yourself for listening to your emotions."*

# Usually...

... Andrew woke up slowly. Today he jerked up right. He'd hoped it was a nightmare. He'd hoped it wasn't true.

But the pregnancy test came back positive.

Oh, you thought I was talking about... Listen, I'm working on this narrating thing.

But yeah, that was a pretty messed up dream. Sadly, it wasn't just a dream either.

Andrew got out of bed and headed over to the bathroom. And there in the mirror was that familiar face.

*You know your mother left because of you. It's all your fault. Had you just been a better son, she would've stuck around.*

*FUCK YOU! You know she left because of YOU! It's all your fault.*

*Ha. You keep telling yourself that.*

*Oh, like hell I will. This is even stupider than that time you made us go looking for a recliner.*

*His father chuckles. Yeah, that was a bit stupid...*

*All I see is trash. Everywhere. Andrew is in a landfill, knee deep in shit.*

*"Stupid, ungrateful asshole," a gruff voice shouts.*

*Andrew thinks of many insults to sling back at the voice but replies with a small grunt. Andrew is 15 now. He's gritting his teeth and biting his tongue and telling himself not to respond.*

I always took Andrew as the sort of guy who didn't take nothing from no one.

*The source of the voice turns out to be a gruff old man, with an equally gruff old bathrobe that seems as if it has as many stains as a thing filled with stains.*

(I apologize for not always thinking so poetically.)

*The gruff old man is Andrew Senior.*

*"Dad, can we go? I don't see any fucking recliners here!" Andrew Junior says indignantly.*

The force of the slap that followed was enough to even make a mark on my face.

*"You wanna eat tonight, boy? Cause we're not fucking leaving without no recliner! I am a hardworking man who puts food on the fucking table and deserves to be able to sit with my feet in the fucking air while watching television!"*

My God, it's a family of potty mouths.

*So the search for a recliner continues in silence with Andrew's father breaking the silence once in a while to explain yet again why he is deserving of such a luxury.*

*Several insults and four slaps later, Andrew's father decides that today just is not the day because the damn privileged upper class decided to hoard their old recliners just to spite him. So, Andrew and his father get into a rundown pickup truck and head home. Home turns out to be in a trailer park on "that" side of town. The side where the bourgeoisie told their children that bad men who wear dirty bathrobes and eat little children live. That side of town.*

*"There's some leftover take-out in the fridge. And get me a beer," Andrew's father grunts to no one in particular, but Andrew understands because he is the only one around. His mother had left years ago. With the baby. But not Andrew.*

*Andrew complies silently, knowing one wrong move could cost him, but is practically screaming in his head how the fat in his father's belly should have enough gravitational pull to get the beer itself.*

*Andrew wolfs down the few remaining dumplings greedily; he wants to have some milk to wash it down, but the milk falls into his dirty cup in several clumps.*

*Andrew looks at the milk with disdain.*

*"Fuckin cheapskate," Andrew's internal voice yells.*

Andrew gazed back in the mirror; his old man grinned back.

*"Yeah, that sucked," he says to him.*

*"Ha! Yeah, it did, didn't it?" he says back to him.*

*"And why was the milk always spoiled? Like, no matter how recently we bought it, it was always coming out like cottage cheese."*

*"Fuckin cottage cheese! Ha!"*

I'm uncertain who was talking to who at this point, but Andrew just looked at the mirror and a small smile began to crack his serious demeanor.

# Chapter 18

# Smiling with his teeth...

... Andrew felt the brisk autumn wind on his face as he walked alongside Andrea. She was going on and on but Andrew was elsewhere.

*Won't this stupid bitch just shut up so I can think?* But he remained silent.

They sat inside a diner and Andrea ordered coffee for the two of them. Andrea was going on and on about the baby this and the baby that and what is she going to do now that she can't drink at Adam's upcoming party and remember that one time she threw up over the side of a bridge and the sound of the vomit hitting the water was disgusting and Andrew are you listening to me?

Andrew blinked.

*Not in the slightest.*

"Yeah."

"Andrew, I'm your girlfriend. We can talk if something is bothering you. I want to help you. I want to be there for you."

Images flashed through Andrew's mind. Voices seared through his brain.

*A woman is crying. She's pregnant. Andrew's father stands over her with a belt.*

*"Stupid self-centered bitch!"*

*The belt snaps through the air and lands with a crack.*

*The woman lets out a little whimper. Andrew looks on through a crack in his door. A single tear rolls down his cheek.*

*But he wipes it away with his sleeve and continues watching.*

"Andrew?! Andrew! I can't believe you haven't been listening to a word I just said!" Andrea shouted. I saw a few patrons glance over out of the corner of Andrew's eye, but he remained transfixed on the single droplet of condensation rolling down the glass between him and Andrea.

Andrew wipes the droplet.

"Nothing. Everything is okay. So, what were you saying about this party?"

# Calmly...

... feel myself evolving.

After much talk of outfits and misfits, Andrew and Andrea walked out of the diner hand in hand. Andrew was still scatterbrained, but he seemed to be pushing most thoughts from his mind.

Andrea pecked him on the cheek and they parted ways.

"See you tonight!" she called after him. "And try to smile!"

Andrew flashed her a smile, but it quickly dissipated when he turned around. His thoughts floated back to the baby.

Andrew needed to clear his head, so he did what his father always did whenever he needed a clear head: drink. And nothing got him in the nostalgic mood like drinking...

*Andrew is still at home. It's a quiet Friday evening in the trailer park. Andrew begins to leave without letting his father know.*

*"Where the hell do you think you're going?" Andrew's father yells after him. Andrew winces.*

*"Dammit. Must've let the door slam," Andrew curses himself.*

"Just going out for a bit, Dad."

"Like hell you are. You aren't going nowhere before I have some good dinner, and it sure as hell won't make itself!"

Andrew walks back to the trailer with his head hung low.

"I don't even know how to cook," he mumbles as he walks past his lumbering father.

"You best start learning."

"Andrea, I'm really sorry! Something unexpected came up. I really was going to be on time," Andrew begs.

They spend the rest of the car ride to Adam's house in silence. Andrea has a nice car, far nicer than anything Andrew could ever afford. He is always coming up with excuses as to why he can't drive her and why she needs to pick him up from random, nondescript locations. Today, it turned out his car is in the shop again because it needs yet another oil change, so Andrea picked him up outside the mechanic.

"Andrew, we've only been going out for a few weeks and you are always late for dates. Do you not care about me?" Andrea asks angrily as they near Adam's house.

Listen up bitch! I have so much shit to deal with, if only you knew the half of it you would be begging for forgiveness right now!

But Andrew never says that aloud. Instead, he remains silent, gazing at the visor mirror, thinking of how alike he and his father look.

*Andrea pulls up to Adam's block and needs to park at the other end because the block is already filled with cars.*

*"Dammit Andrew! You see how late you made us?"*

*There it is again. That word. Us. Andrew has an us to be a part of. It might be fragile, it may be weak, but it is an us, nonetheless.*

*Andrea quickly forgives Andrew as they walk up to the door and grabs his hand.*

*The music is very loud. Too loud for Andrew's thoughts to be heard even by himself. Adam gives Andrew a hug as soon as he sees him.*

*"Welcome buddy! About time you showed up. And nice shoes you got there," Adam shouts above the din.*

*Andrew turns red. They are Adam's shoes. Adam knows it too. They had just given them to Andrew a few days ago.*

*Andrew's mind begins to conjure up several retorts to Adam's comment, most of which contain one or more explicit terms. Andrew went with the shortest option.*

*"Thanks."*

*Andrea whisks Andrew away to the drinks table.*

*"Get me something that makes me feel sophisticated," Andrea says. Andrew knows exactly what she wants.*

Andrew pops open the cork on a bottle of whiskey.

*Pop! went the cork as his father pours some whiskey into a glass. The amber liquid flows steadily, and it reminds Andrew of the apple juice his mother used to give him before she....*

*"Son, a boy becomes a man when he has his first drink. My old man gave me mine when I was 12, so I figured I'd do the same with my own. It'll sting at first, but you'll come to learn that it softens the sting of other things. Drink up."*

*Twelve year old Andrew holds the glass up to his face, the smell making his eyes water.*

*Just like apple juice from Mom.*

*Andrew lifts the cup to his lips and takes a swig. It burns his throat. He wants to gag, he wants to spit it out, but he knows that if he does anything besides for swallow, he'll get a beating. So he blinks away the tears and gulps it down.*

*"Atta boy," his father murmurs as he slides back into his chair, contempt with teaching his son something useful.*

Andrew hands Andrea her glass. She's bragging to a bunch of her friends how chivalrous Andrew is. Andrew just sipped his drink.

Several shots later, Andrew's vision begins to blur. Music blasting, people dancing and shouting, and Andrew sits on the couch, nursing his drink. Adam plops down next to him.

"Heyyy, Andrew! Buddy! My man... How you liking my shoes? They serving you well?"

*A few people nearby hear and glance down at Andrew's shoes.*

*"The fuck you talking about?" Andrew hastily responds, trying to cover up Adam's blunder.*

*"You know, I gave you those cause I am oh so generous to those less fortunate than I. Those poor, unfortunate souls. Well, in your case, I guess just poor and unfortunate," Adam slurs.*

*"Get it? Because gingies have no soul!" Adam high fives the nearest guy.*

*Andrew knows that Adam is wasted. But that doesn't make him any less pissed.*

*"Man, you're fucking wasted," Andrew says, then loud enough for those around who heard what Adam said, "He has no idea what he's saying."*

*Andrew then quickly gets up from the couch, leaving the drunken Adam behind.*

*Andrew feels like he needs another drink.*


*After much slow drifting from point to point, mingling with different crowds, and several more alcoholic beverages (some of which Andrew didn't even know what they contained), Andrew finally finds himself next to Andrea.*

*She reeks of booze and is stumbling around, giggling at everything and at nothing.*

*"Andrew! Hey, hey-* "then she says loud enough for everyone in the vicinity to hear, *"Andrew is the best freaking boyfriend in the world!"*

*I've never seen Andrea drunk before. I mean, Andrew has never seen her drunk before.*

*Before I have any time to ponder what just happened, Andrea desperately reaches for Andrew's hand, misses, grabs his forearm, and marches him upstairs.*

*Andrea half leads, half stumbles into one of the many unoccupied bedrooms. She shoves Andrew inside and slams the door shut behind her.*

*"Andrew, I want a family,"* she says, her tone changing drastically from moments before.

*"I want to have a family with you. Andrew, I feel so alone. It's just me and my mom..."* She is on the verge of tears now.

*"Andrew, I want a baby."*

*She was crying now, a downpour of tears drenching her shirt.*

*Andrew sits there, stone-faced.*

*Andrew wipes the tear from his face and continues watching. His mother cowering on the floor, hand clutching her stomach which is beginning to form a small bump.*

*Andrew's father stands over her, belt in hand.*

*"What the fuck do you mean you want a baby? I can't afford another kid! I am a hardworking man, I make the*

money around here, I put food on the table, I make the de-cisions around here, and I am deciding that you are getting rid of it!"

"Please, just think! This is your child!" Andrew's mother begs.

"Well, if this one will be a worthless, money burning little shit like the other one," he points towards Andrew's door, "then I don't want it either!"

"Andrew, please- "but she is cut short by the whooshing of the belt through the air. She lets out a small whimper.

"Either you get that baby out of here or you get out of here with that baby!" Andrew's father snarls.

Andrew lets out the smallest of cries at that proposition, but it is loud enough for his father to hear. His father's head snaps towards Andrew's door and sees Andrew peeking through the crack.

"Get out here, boy!"

Andrew shuffles quickly to push the drawer in front of the door, but his father is quicker. Andrew shuffles out of his room, his head hanging dejectedly, being dragged by his arm.

His father grabs him by the chin and yanks his head up.

"Look at me when I talk to you! Now, do you feel bad for this bitch?"

Andrew doesn't respond. SLAP!

*"I said, do you feel bad for this bitch?"*

*Silence. WHACK!*

*"DO," WHACK!*

*"YOU," WHACK!*

*"FEEL," WHACK!*

*"BAD," WHACK!*

*"FOR," WHACK!*

*"HER?" WHACK!*

*"No, sir," Andrew whispers*

*"See babe," Andrew's father says to the woman on the floor, "Even this dumb shit gets it. I make the money, I make the rules. I am so generous to put a roof over your head, to put food on the table, and then you have the fucking audacity to ask me to provide for another person! I think you need to be educated in how to show proper gratitude. See, my son here has already been educated. Been educatin' him since the day my beloved wife brought him into this world. The day that she sacrificed herself to bring him into this world. She went through so much pain just so he could live, so I had to teach him to be grateful. I had to show him what she went through. Been teachin' him his whole life. And there ain't no greater pleasure than a man seeing his own son teachin' someone else what he taught. Son, why don't you educate this dear woman on showing proper gratitude?"*

*Andrew's father holds out the belt.*

*"I said educate her, dammit!"*

*Andrew takes the belt.*

*"Now teach boy!"*

*Andrew halfheartedly swings the belt at her.*

*"If the lesson is going to stick, she'll need the marks to last."*

*Andrew swings the belt again, this time a little harder. She lets out a little gasp as the belt makes contact.*

*"Harder!"*

*This time the belt made a mark.*

*"HARDER!"*

*A droplet of blood rolls down her cheek from the cut the belt had made. Andrew wipes the blood off her cheek.*
*Then he swings again.*

*Andrew blinks back into reality. Andrea is crying on the bed, wailing about how she wants a family, how she wants a baby, how Andrew is being a self-centered bastard for not wanting to help her.*

*Maybe it's the alcohol, maybe it's the anger, maybe it's the loneliness, but whatever it is, when Andrew peers past Andrea and sees the mirror on the wall, he sees how remarkably alike he and his father look. And he realizes something.*

*This bitch needs to be educated.*

*At that moment, another couple stumbles into the room.*

*"Oops. Didn't mean to- interrupt," one of them slurs.*

*And just like that Andrew's anger abates, quickly drains out of him.*

Andrew sat in the corner, nursing his drink. He got a text from Andrea.

*"hey, can we continue that convo? come to my place ASAP."*

Andrew stared blankly at the phone.

*This time, no one will be there to interrupt.*

Andrew drained the last of his drink and stood up.

# Chapter 20

# Odiously, my eyes shot open...

... _my_ eyes.

Oh God. Oh God. I needed to do something about this. I needed to help Andrea before Andrew hurt her. I needed to-

But then I looked around me, at the wallpaper peeling off the walls, the plaster falling from the ceiling, the colors fading from the poster on the back of the door, and the window seemed even smaller than before.

That's when I reminded myself of who I was, who I really was. I wasn't Andrew, I wasn't some sort of hero. I was powerless. I couldn't possibly help her. I was a nobody.

But recently, I had felt like a somebody. I saw into Andrew's life and maybe, just maybe, I saw myself having a chance. And for the first time in forever, I second guessed myself. I doubted my inabilities. And I reached for the doorknob before I changed my mind.

# Ghoulishly...

... I reached for the doorknob, took a deep breath, and pushed it open. I was by Andrea's home and I saw that she didn't lock the door after letting Andrew in. Well, Andrew saw after she let him in, and I saw through Andrew.

The things that I heard going through his mind frighten me to this very day.

I noticed the mirror in the entranceway was cracked. It looked like someone punched it.

I heard them before I saw them; I heard crying.

Andrea was cowering in the corner, head tucked between her knees, body quivering from her sobbing.

She looked up at me, her red eyes begging for help.

That's when I noticed Andrew's hulking figure, sitting on the edge of the bed. His head was in his hands, digging his fingers into his scalp. I heard him mutter under his breath, "Dad, what the hell have you made me into?"

The three of us remained transfixed for several moments, Andrea sitting in the corner, Andrew on the edge of the bed, and me standing stupidly in the doorway.

"Andrea, are you-," I started to say, but before I could finish asking her if she was alright, Andrea stood up. I could see the marks on her arms. I also noticed a small bruise on her cheek.

Then she did something very unexpected.

"What the fuck are you doing?" she asked.

"I-"

"Get the fuck out of my house!"

"Andrea-"

"Get away from us!"

Odd. There was that word again. Us.

"What the hell are you still doing here?" she shrieked as I just stood in the doorway, dumbfounded.

"Andrea, I swear I wasn't spying on you guys. Just when I saw what Andrew was about to do to you, I couldn't just stand by and watch."

"So you were watching us?!"

"No, I-"

But how should I have responded? How could I possibly have explained to her?

"Get. Out. Now."

Andrew looked up for the first time, and I could see the

tears in his eyes. I could see the scars of his past, of his present. I saw all the pain, the confusion, the anger bottled up for years. I could see his education.

Andrew put his head back in his hands and resumed muttering about how he was so sorry.

"Out, fucking creep!" Andrea shouted, her sadness and confusion now completely replaced with fury.

So I retreated back out the doorway I had just come through, leaving exactly the same way that I had entered.

# Chapter 22

# Idiot...

... how could I have been so fucking stupid?

I cursed myself.

I punched the wall.

I cried out in pain, both from the situation and from the punch to the wall. I stifled my cries by plunging my head into my pillow.

I tried. I tried to make something of myself. I tried to help somebody.

What the hell was I thinking? How could I have been so stupid? I should've known that I would've only made things worse.

I peered through Andrew's eyes for a few moments.

He was still in the room in Andrea's home. I could feel the cool tears running down his hot face. He and Andrea were hugging.

He kept whispering, "I'm so sorry, I'm so sorry," and Andrea kept shushing him.

I couldn't stand this for a moment longer and I returned to the familiar, lonely, darkness of my room. I could feel the walls closing in on me.

I closed my eyes, waiting for the numbness of sleep to wash over me and drag the pain away with it.

## Sleep

Sleep be not a barrier, but a tool.

Hinder me not, for I am a fool.

Neither abused nor addicted, but an aid,

To assist my aims which are beaten and frayed.


Sleep, whisk me away.

With my options weighed, my decision's made.

I wish to run away with you, away from addiction;

To where skies are blue, saved from affliction.


Sleep complies and closes my eyes;

Sadness slips away.

Numbness is mistaken for bliss,

And there I remain, nothing amiss.

# Chapter 23

# Through the looking glass...

... was where I remained.

I hadn't been galivanting in Andrew's body. I just couldn't bring myself to. Not after what I saw. I couldn't unsee it, and I didn't want to experience it again.

I know, I know. Crazy, right? Me admitting that someone else's life is worse than mine. Who would've seen that one coming?

But it was okay. I had moved on.

So, Andrew's life wasn't all that I thought it was cut out to be. That didn't make my life any better. That didn't get anyone to notice me. I was still the same old me.

It was slightly comforting to know that I was grateful for not being one person on this planet. But not that comforting.

I'd been thinking about who I would like to occupy next. God, I sound like a leech. I couldn't go back to my old life.

I could be anyone, but clearly, I didn't want to be just anyone.

Andrew was lonely. He always felt lonely, even when he was with others. He wasn't too bright. His father was abusive. His mother was MIA. He had a few friends. Some serious relationship issues. And he was poor.

Now, I was just toying with this idea, but if I had a negative experience with him, I should've been looking for his polar opposite in order to have a positive experience. I needed somebody who wasn't lonely. Somebody without poor excuses for parents. Somebody who had plenty of friends. Somebody who everybody loved. Somebody who wasn't poor...

# Opulently...

... I felt the wind whipping at my face before my eyes even opened. The world was tinted sepia through the lenses of the sunglasses that were resting on the bridge of Adam's nose.

They adjusted the rearview mirror while ripping down the road, wind running through their hair, music blaring in their convertible orange muscle car.

Damn, they knew how to run in style.

I could see out of their peripheral vision that there were three people in the car with them: Altair (their boyfriend), Akira (their best friend), and Alicia (their other best friend). Everyone was smiling and laughing and singing along to the music. This was exactly what I needed.

Despite the cold winter air, Adam had the roof down. It felt incredible. The icy air whipping at their face, landscapes flashing by in a blurry collage of colors, and all their favorite people in the world right next to them.

Adam was happy. And so was I.

Altair said he had to meet his family at the diner. Akira and Alicia needed to do some studying at the library for a project they were partners on together.

Adam glumly complied, annoyed that they wouldn't be able to spend the rest of the afternoon with their friends.

They dropped the three of them off at the corner of the diner, because Akira and Alicia said they wouldn't mind walking to the library. Adam kissed Altair goodbye and waved Akira and Alicia off.

Adam began to drive away, leaving the music blasting. I realized now that I couldn't even hear Adam think. The music was just so loud, like by their party. The static was just so loud in their head, and the only words I could make out were singing along to the music. I didn't think much of it.

Adam drove on, unsure of where they wanted to go. They circled around for a bit. Why wouldn't they go home?

After several minutes of cruising, Adam drove to the library.

*"They sure as hell better be there,"* they thought as soon as they turned off the car's engine.

It was the first cohesive thought I heard from them the entire time.

Adam walked up the steps to the library, a mixture of anxiousness and anger forming a pit in their stomach.

"Excuse me," they said to the librarian, "did two people walk in here a few minutes ago? A guy and a girl? He's kinda tall and dopey and she was wearing a red hoodie?

The librarian thought for a moment, put on their spectacles, scratched their head, and seemed to be racking their elderly brain for some distant memory of days long gone.

Adam grew impatient.

"I don't believe so," the librarian said in a ghost-quiet whisper.

"Goddamn," Adam muttered to themselves as they walked away, shaking their head.

"Language, sonny," the librarian said in another ghost-quiet whisper.

Adam was too dejected to correct them.

Adam was filled with dread as they walked towards their car, wondering where Akira and Alicia were.

"They sure as hell better not be- "Adam thought to themselves as they raced down the street, but their worst fear was confirmed. There was Akira and Alicia sitting in a booth in the diner, laughing. And sitting across from them was Altair.

"Fucking assholes!" Adam cursed out loud as they drove towards their house.

*"I'm sure there must be some sort of explanation for this. Yeah, maybe Altair's family didn't show up yet. Yeah, that's what it is! And Akira and Alicia decided to grab a bite before going to study. That must be what it is!"* Adam reasoned with himself.

They kept repeating this refrain in their mind, desperately searching for a way to merit their friends. Those who they referred to as their friends.

Adam turned the music on higher, hoping to drown out the sound of their worries.

I didn't think this was possible, but Adam's house was even nicer by day when there wasn't any party going on. The long driveway circulated around a marble fountain. The large wooden double doors led into a beautifully furnished house, with wooden flooring and leather couches and expensive looking sculptures everywhere.

While shuffling down the hallway, I couldn't help but notice how quiet the house was. Adam made his way into the kitchen and the wonderful smell of a gourmet dinner wafted through the air.

I expected to see Adam's mother cooking, but it was a butler.

"Hey Alfred," Adam said to the middle-aged man. Adam liked him. When they saw him, their mood alleviated a bit. Their worry was suppressed.

"Oh, hello Adam," Alfred replied over his shoulder, not taking his eyes off the pot before him. "Your parents said I should let you know that something unexpected came up and they needed to stay for just a few more days. They should be back by Monday."

Adam's heart stuttered.

*"Classic stuck-up pricks who don't give two shits about their own child. Business my ass. They just want to be away from me because I'm a freak,"* Adam screamed in their head. But all they said to Alfred was, "Oh, I'm not hungry."

Adam rushed out of the kitchen, mind swirling with dread about their parents, their friends, their boyfriend. While walking up the stairs, Adam wished Alfred would come after them, comfort them, parent them more than his parents ever would. But he didn't.

Adam trudged down the hallway, which looked all too familiar to me, and went into their room.

Their four-poster bed was adjacent to their polished mahogany desk, complete with a walnut-colored leather office chair. And don't get me started on their closet. I had never seen so much clothing in my entire life, besides for in a department store.

Adam was unimpressed. I guess they were just used to it.

Adam pulled on a pair of expensive headphones and listened to music to stave off thoughts about their parents and friends.

Adam skulked around, only pausing the music, when they heard a knock on their door a little while later. They opened the door to find piping hot dinner on a tray placed on the floor right outside of their room.

"Thank God for Alfred," they murmured.

After eating dinner (which just so happened to be some of the best tasting food I have ever tasted), doing work, and moping to some depressing music, Adam finally just sat in bed and stared out the window. It was beginning to drizzle, the rain droplets pattering against the glass.

Adam poked their head out the door and heard Alfred humming across the house. Then they returned to their closet and pulled a shoe box from the back of their closet. Inside, there was a plastic bag filled with drugs.

Adam remained in their room for the next few hours, thinking about how incredible it was that an entire band could fit inside their headphones and play music for them on demand.

# Enthusiastically...

... Adam opened their eyes. They're sitting with Altair. The aroma of freshly brewed coffee wafted across the café. The dark wooden tables were all filled with patrons talking and laughing. Adam was pleased with the noise.

"So, what are you thinking for the party?" Altair said loudly so they can be heard above the noise.

Adam sat quietly for a moment. Thoughts of Altair sitting across from Akira and Alicia at the diner flash through their mind. They grimace for a moment.

"Don't worry. If you build it, they will come."

"What the heck is that supposed to mean?"

"Field of-? Ah, never mind."

Altair stared at Adam blankly.

"Are you feeling okay?" Altair began, "because you've been acting strange recently."

*"That's because you and Akira and Alicia are a bunch of backstabbing-"*

"Yeah. I'm fine."

Adam dropped Altair off at their house, pecked them on the cheek, and told them they would see them tomorrow night at the party.

Adam then promptly turned the music on full volume as they drove off. It was almost like they didn't want to hear what they're thinking. What could they possibly not want to hear?

Adam did the same thing as yesterday. They threw their bag on the floor, shirked off their shoes, and shuffled into the kitchen.

"Hey Alfred."

"Hello Adam. How was your day?"

"Same old."

And that was it. That was where the conversation ended. Adam wished that he would continue the conversation, that he would press them. But he never did. Why would he want to? Adam was just his boss's kid.

He didn't know how much he meant to them. He may have only made him dinner because he was paid to, but he was the only one making them dinner.

Adam's mother never made them dinner.

While Alfred was finishing up cooking, Adam sat at the table, eating the freshly baked cookies that Alfred was famous for. The soft, warm, scrumptious bites brought Adam back to his childhood.

*Adam is sitting at the very same table. His feet are dangling from the edge of the chair, swinging, while he devours Alfred's cookies. They love how he hums while he cooks. They could listen to him forever.*

*"Eat up," he says as he puts spaghetti and meatballs with marinara sauce onto china. Then, he walks off to clean some other part of the house. That's when the silence consumes Adam.*

*Adam can feel the emptiness. The large house suddenly feels never ending. And the silence. It is deafening. It is a constant reminder of how alone Adam is.*

*The silence shouts in their ear how their parents don't care about them, how they were always gone because they didn't want to be around them, how they didn't love them.*

*Whenever Alfred leaves the room, they feel like they have lost the only person who has ever loved them. They would also feel pathetic that the only person who loved them is paid to do so. But it didn't make a difference to them. Even his feigned love and care is better than nothing.*

"Eat up," Alfred said as he served Adam dinner. He hummed as he walked out of the room, off to go do his job. His humming faded as he walked further away, leaving Adam alone with the silence.

# Religiously...

... Adam was sitting with Altair, Akira, and Alicia in their car.

"So, can you guys help me prepare for the party tonight?"

All three started providing excuses immediately.

"Sorry, my mom wants me home."

"Yeah, mine too."

"I, uh, need to finish up some work."

Adam rubbed their eyes with their hand, attempting to cover their grimace.

*"They honestly don't think I fucking know the difference."*

"Alright, whatever. See you tonight."

The three of them exited the car and Adam was only accompanied by the silence.

Adam stopped by the convenience store to pick up some essentials. While loading their basket with all sorts of delicacies, their mind began to wander.

They thought about their parents, their friends, their past friends, oh these are good potato chips, what was he going to do with his life, need that salsa, definitely going to play that song tonight, and all sort of things that float through one's mind while walking aimlessly down the snack aisle.

When rounding the corner, Adam saw something that made them stop dead in their tracks. They couldn't catch their breath for a moment. Suddenly, they found it was difficult to focus on anything. They felt faint.

It was Antonio.

What did Adam have to do with him? But I got the answer I was looking for all too quickly. Images flashed through Adam's mind. Sitting alone at a table. Antonio saying hello. Friendship. Hugs. Hands. Hatred.

*Adam watches their parents walk out the door, suitcases in tow.*

*"See you in a week, honey!" their mother shouts as she closes the door behind her.*

*"And good luck in school!"*

*Adam and their parents just moved to the neighborhood that summer. Adam doesn't know anyone around here. It didn't help that they were also a quiet kid. As the final weeks of summer drag on, Adam hasn't made any friends. They all seem to have their friends already. Why would they want Adam to join?*

*Adam thought the new manservant, Alfred, seems kind. There are kind people in this world.*

*Alfred always makes him a yummy dinner and they love it when he hums. It makes the house not feel so empty. But*

*Adam knows that they can't be friends with him; he was much older than Adam and plus he was only nice to Adam because Adam's parents paid him.*

*So Adam was alone.*

*Their first week at school is spent alone.*

*He doesn't speak to anyone in the hallways. He sits alone at lunch. Adam thinks that they would simply spend the rest of their life alone, unloved.*

*Everything changes one day, when a boy sits down next to him at lunch. The boy introduces himself as Antonio. Adam thinks that Antonio is the most interesting person in the entire world. Antonio loved to draw, watch anime, talk to old people, do yoga, talk about the meaning of life, and all sorts of other quirky things.*

*Adam thinks Antonio is brilliant. Antonio doesn't care what other people think of him. He does what he wants when he wants to.*

*Adam envies that freedom.*

*As the year goes on, Adam and Antonio grow very close. They have sleepovers and share secrets with each other and say screw the rest of the world.*

*Antonio's family takes Adam in like one of their own. Adam comes over for dinner all the time and often spends the night, not wanting to go back to his empty house.*

*Antonio's family is very interesting. They are all very strong-minded individuals who shout at the dinner table* and never say please or thank you and they all love each other. Adam loves it.

Adam's dinner table is always quiet and fraught with stupid small talk and ridiculous amounts of politeness.
Adam feels at home with Antonio's family.

These are some of the best days Adam has in recent memory. He never had parents who cared for him, or a friend he could rely on, and Antonio provides both of those for Adam.

One fateful evening, Antonio tells Adam a secret that will change their relationship forever.

"Adam, I'm- I..."

But Adam already knows. Or at least, he thinks he knows.

"Adam, I... secretly made my own trading card game. With illustrations and stats and abilities and everything."

Well, that took a sharp left turn.

"Oh, and by the way, I'm gay."

Adam hugs Antonio and tells him that it doesn't make a difference in the world to them. They will be best friends forever. Adam and Antonio versus The World.

After Antonio comes out to Adam, their relationship changes overnight.

Adam thinks it is for the better.

Adam and Antonio talk all night long about who they have a crush on in the class. They go through the entire list, Anto-

*nio listing each of their best features.*

*"He has a great jawline."*

*"He has great biceps."*

*Then Antonio drops a bomb.*

*"Adam, you're pretty hot."*

*Adam doesn't know what to say. He's never been complimented before.*

*"Really, you think so?"*

*"Yeah, you're like one of the hottest people in the class."*

*Adam blushes, thinking it is cute that their best friend thinks they are good looking.*

*Several weeks later, Adam is staying by Antonio's house. Adam is laying in bed and Antonio sits down on the edge of the bed like always. In this very formation, Adam lying against the bedrest and Antonio sitting crisscrossed at the foot of the bed, the two of them solve all the world's problems. They speak about everything like this, facing each other.*

*On this night, Antonio tells Adam to scoot over because they were going to watch The Shining together.*

*Adam is completely used to these antics and doesn't think twice about it. About halfway through, Adam feels something on his leg. It is Antonio's leg. Antonio is slowly wrapping his leg over Adam's in a very casual manner.*

*Adam casts a glance sideways towards Antonio's face, but*

*Antonio remains transfixed on the screen, not showing the slightest indication that anything is up.*

*Adam begins to feel very uncomfortable as Antonio's leg crosses further and further over Adam's own. Eventually, Adam gets up and mumbles something about needing to use the bathroom. When he returns, Adam sits on the opposite side of the bed.*

*This repeats itself several times over the next few weeks. Every time Adam shrugs it off like it is nothing and he simply excuses himself when Antonio goes too far.*

*They never discuss what went on then. Adam can't tell if Antonio doesn't realize Adam's discomfort or simply doesn't care. Adam hopes for the former.*

*He doesn't dare say anything to Antonio, his best friend, his only friend. What if Antonio gets upset with him? What if Antonio doesn't let him sleep at his house anymore? Adam would be forced to sleep at their own house, alone, or worse, with their parents.*

*So, Adam never says anything. They just let it slide.*

*Anyways, they reason with their self, they would never let Antonio take it too far. They will simply stop it if they ever feel it gets too heated. Adam thinks he can handle this.*

*Somewhere along in the school year, Adam's parents leave for vacation without even letting them know. They leave a message with Alfred to tell Adam when they got home from school that they will be back in two weeks.*

*Adam is happy about this because it means they get to stay* at Antonio's house, but they can't deny their anger at their parents for not even letting them know. They think they deserve at least that much.

So, when Adam arrives at Antonio's house that evening, they are in a rather sour mood. They feel the world has cheated them. They feel that life is terrible. And when Antonio begins to hug them, Adam feels helpless. They feel like there is nothing they can do in their life.

Adam feels like they are alone in the world.

Adam is too weak that night to stop Antonio.

They don't have the strength to get up and leave.

They just sit there and take it.

All of it.

Antonio's hands start on Adam's back in an embrace, but they slowly but surely work their way lower, and lower down Adam's back.

Antonio's long fingers run softly over Adam's biceps and shoulders and chest, intricately tracing Adam's skin.

Adam begins to cry silently. The tears slowly drip down their face, as Antonio's hands slowly work their way down their body.

Adam feels helpless. They feel used. They feel like an object. They feel like there is nothing they could possibly do in this world. They are powerless.

Antonio's hands work their way onto Adam's thighs. Antonio

*has his eyes closed and a slight grin on his face.*

*After being caressed and touched all over for some time, Adam ejaculates.*

*Then they begin to sob uncontrollably.*

*Adam gets to their senses and stands up to leave.*

*"Where are you going?" Antonio croons.*

*Adam mumbles something about going to shower.*

*"I don't want to shower. I don't want to wash the Adam off me."*

*Adam doesn't say a word. He just continues walking out the door, and just as he is about to close the door, Antonio calls out, "Would you like to spend the night, Adam?"*

*Adam shuts the door behind them.*

*Adam doesn't speak to Antonio after that night.*

*Antonio tries to corner Adam in the hallway, sit next to them by lunch, anything to try to converse with Adam. But Adam remains silent the entire time.*

*Adam feels broken inside. The one thing they had in the world, the only person whom they loved and loved them back, had betrayed them.*

*Something broke inside of Adam that night. Something which could never be fixed.*

Andrew blinked back into reality. They were filled with disgust. They wanted to break something.

Adam hadn't seen Antonio since they had switched schools yet again. They also hadn't spoken to him since.

Like they always did in the past whenever they saw Antonio's face, they turned around and quickly walked in the other direction, eager to put as much distance between them as possible.

Adam finished shopping for the party and returned home to begin setting up.

None of their friends were able to help them. They all had excuses.

Antonio also had excuses why he did what he did.

Adam tried to shove the thought away from their head, desperately not wanting to associate their current friends with their previous one.

Adam had tried to make a new name after transferring schools. Adam wouldn't make the same mistake twice. Nobody could be trusted.

Adam resumed setting up in silence, their only trusty companion which seemed to stick with them through and through.

Later that evening, the crowds started trickling in.

Eventually, Altair, Akira, and Alicia strolled in. They apologized for not being able to help Adam out before.

Adam didn't believe a word that came out of their mouths.

The night went on. Music blasted. Shots were poured. Joints were shared. But Adam wasn't having a good time. Just seeing the people they called friends left a sour taste in their mouth.

I noticed Andrew and Andrea showed up separately. Andrew had told Adam that he and Andrea had a falling out. Andrew didn't tell Adam, but I think I had a pretty good idea. Probably something to do with the fact that Andrea was wearing long sleeves that night.

Adam wasn't drinking that night. They tried to laugh and joke around, but they couldn't get their mind off Antonio.

Adam never wanted to feel that way again. They never wanted to feel abused. Feel used.

*After they stopped going to Antonio's house, Adam is forced to spend more time at home. Home usually has a population of two: Adam and Alfred.*

*Adam's parents are always off galivanting, travelling the world for "business". But Adam doesn't mind. Alfred becomes their father and mother. Alfred doesn't even know how much he means to Adam. His cooking. His humming. His random sage advice. Adam loves it all.*

*But they know that he only tolerates Adam because he is paid to do so.*

*Adam realizes then that if that's what it takes to have somebody care about you, then they would do just that.*

*As soon as they switch to their new school, Adam comes with a plan. It may sound rudimentary, elementary, and juvenile, but Adam knows it will work.*

*So, Adam starts by giving Andrew, the coolest guy around, a pair of sneakers.*

*Adam tries to seem altruistic about it, and they were confident that Andrew has fallen for it.*

*Adam then continues this trend. They shower people they want to be friends with, with gifts. They give Altair a bottle of cologne, Akira a diamond-studded choker, and Alicia one of their mother's handbags.*

*They all instantly fall in love with this new rich kid.*

*Adam starts gaining attention in school. People stop ignoring them. The silence is replaced with noise. And when the noise begins to subside, Adam simply pays their friends even more.*

*Adam feels loved, even though they know it is only because he pays them to love them.*

*That's why Adam always throws parties; it fills the emptiness.*

*That's why Adam always blasts the music; it stifles the silence.*

*This party too, is merely to make some noise.*

Adam strolled lazily around the party, the lone sober soul in a sea of drunks. Adam saw many faces, they all seemed so happy, so content. Adam felt so alone.

I was confused: how could Adam feel lonely? They had so many people who would kill to be a part of their crew. How could someone like that feel alone?

I couldn't understand it, until Adam showed me.

Adam was wandering alone when they came across a very drunk Altair, Akira, and Alicia. They were sitting on a couch entertaining a whole crowd. The crow laughed raucously.

"-and then Adam just let himself get raped by this guy in his old school!" Altair bellowed.

The crowd laughed and crowed. None of them saw Adam peering around the corner.

Akira continued, "Even better, you should see the way he wipes Andrew's poor ass. See, Adam wanted to make some friends because he was a lonely ass loser in his old school, so he started giving Andrew free clothing. He'd probably suck Andrew's balls like he did to Antonio if it meant he would have a friend!"

Everyone was roaring in laughter. Adam remained hidden and silent, but they were not quiet in their head.

Adam's eye began to water.

Alicia piped up, "You know why he went to that kid's house in the first place? It's because his parents hate his fucking guts more than we do and they ditch him and go on vacation. That's why this house is always open for parties, because his folks never want to be around him!"

Akira continued, "But hey, I'll put up with his lame, queer ass if it means I get free stuff and VIP access to all of his parties, which by the way, you guys know he only throws because he's trying to buy you too."

The crowd didn't laugh at that last remark. Neither did Adam.

Adam wiped away their tears and did the same thing they did when they saw Antonio: they turned around and walked away as quickly as possible.

Adam didn't want to admit it was true. I saw in Adam's mind that The Roast of Adam had been a regular event at their parties.

They didn't realize that Adam knew. Adam would never dare tell them. Adam couldn't bear the thought of losing them too.

Adam didn't want to be alone. Not anymore. They'd had enough of the silence. They'd had enough of the loneliness. Adam no longer cared where the noise or the company came from, as long as it was there.

So, Adam let this go on. Adam let them have their fun if it meant they would have someone to call their friends.

Adam walked back inside his own house, alone in a sea of people, hearing only the quiet in the cacophony.

**The Silence**

The silence of fear,

The silence of fright,

The silence of all that goes bump in the night.


The silence of love,

The silence of laughter,

The silence of joy and all that comes after.


The silence of family,

The silence of friends,

The silence of good which knows no ends.


The silence of darkness,

The silence of death,

The silence of my dear Elizabeth.

# God...

... I opened my eyes. My eyes.

I was back in my room.

How could Adam live like that? How could anyone live like that?

I certainly couldn't, and I was grateful that I had the option not to.

I saw too much of myself in Adam. It may have expressed itself differently, but they were just as lonely as I was.

In a way, Adam was lonelier. They may disagree with me on this, but I believe that no love is better than fake love.

I sat up in bed feeling disgusted. The injustice of Adam's situation weighed on me like his entire house was on my shoulders.

He did bring it upon himself, but who can blame him?

The next few weeks were a haze of identity roulette. Every day or two I would try on a new body, only to find something wrong.

He was anorexic. She had panic attacks. This family was rotten. Everyone had problems. Soon enough, I couldn't walk around without just seeing one big problem, everywhere. Everyone's lives were just filled with crap. I couldn't even look at people without seeing their problems instead of their faces.

Andrew became more and more closed off as the year went on. It was subtle, but I noticed it. I found it increasingly difficult to not see his father's face when I saw him.

Adam continuously kissed up to those around him. I could see the pain hidden behind his façade of suaveness. He just went on, trying to buy people. I'm sure he will come to the realization one day that love cannot be bought, only cultivated. I hope I'm not around to see it.

I became more depressed than usual. More reserved than I already was. How could this world be filled with so much pain so much suffering?

Yet, behind it all, as much as I glimpsed into other's lives, as much as I saw their flaws, I still felt their troubles paled in comparison to mine. I felt that if push came to shove, I could probably survive in their skin. Being that I had the choice not to be me, I opted out.

They don't know my suffering. They couldn't possibly. Only I can.

As I went through person after person, I became less excited and more dreadful as to how they will disappoint. Everyone did in the end. At least, that's what I thought, until I decided to try one person on for size.

I had a bit of resentment because of how she treated me on that fateful night when I had a peek at the dark side of the walking time bomb that is Andrew. I guess that's why it took me so long to try her out.

Beggars can't be choosers, and I'm running out of options, and fast.

So, Andrea, here goes nothing.

# Omniscience.

Vanilla. Its strong scent made Andrea's nose twitch.

Andrea was in her bedroom. She was doing her hair in the mirror while humming to herself. Just like Alfred.

"Andrea! Come down for dinner," a woman's voice called.

"Comin' Mom."

Andrea finished braiding her hair and took one final look at herself in the mirror. She felt her stomach, where Andrew's baby had once been.

Her room had plush purple carpet. Hung on the walls were several awards and certificates of achievement. Her gold ac-cented desk held *The Princess Bride* by S. Morgenstern and several trophies. I noticed that many of them are for first, second, or even third, place.

Man, this girl seemed good at everything. Honor roll. Soccer championship MVP in the game that she lost! Spelling Bee finalist. Science fair honorable mention.

I guessed her flaw wasn't in academics or sports. I would just have to wait and see what was wrong with her. There was always something wrong.

Andrea went downstairs to the kitchen. I could definitely rule out any sort of financial problems just from looking around her house.

I heard several people laughing. It was coming from the kitchen.

"Oh, Alex. You are quite the comedian," Andrea's father says, his freckled face scrunched up in a grin.

Alex was Andrea's little brother.

It sounded almost- joyful?- in there. I was taken aback; Andrea didn't seem to be. As a matter of fact, as Andrea walked into the kitchen, the only thing she was- was happy. Pure, unadulterated, happiness.

I was just waiting for it to come, her problem. It would show itself soon. I just knew it. It always did.

But it didn't. I was getting nervous. It couldn't possibly be, could it?

Andrea sat down at the dinner table and her family was just so- happy.

Her mother served a delicious dinner of gumbo. Andrea and Alex told their parents how their days were. Her father said work was a bit stressful today, but nothing he couldn't handle. Her mother just gave everyone words of encouragement and plenty of love.

This was unnerving. I wasn't sure why. It was almost unbelievable.

I spent the remainder of the weekend observing Andrea.

Her life wasn't perfect, but it was damn near. She had her struggles, but nothing too bad.

Andrew was nothing more than a fading scar, a blemish of some distant pain which would surely disappear entirely some time soon.

She was smart, but not so smart that it filled her with existential dread. She was pretty, but not so pretty that people would abuse her. She was popular, but not so popular that she couldn't know who her real friends were. She (mostly) got along with her little brother.

Andrea seemed too good to be true.

It was just a day before the holidays that Andrea's problem revealed itself to me.

I knew it would. Eventually.

I'll admit, I was a bit disappointed. I thought Andrea was different. I guess no one is.

It's funny how three little words can change a person's entire life.

*It is the day holiday vacation begins.*

I had just sidled up in my hidey hole with a week's worth of IV fluid.

Andrea walks into her house after school had been dismissed for break and her parents were sitting on the couch.

"Andrea, baby. We have to talk," her father begins.

"Sure, what's going on?"

"Andrea, you know we love you with all of our heart," her mother says, ignoring her question.

"Yeah, but Mom, what is this all about?" Andrea looks into her mother's deep, dark, loving eyes.

"Andrea, you're adopted."

Three little words. Three little words which can cause so much pain. Such a simple phrase which can make a world of a difference.

I feel a little piece of Andrea break.

Andrea opens her mouth, but no words come out.

"I know baby, it's a lot. But we love you."

Andrea's mother and father- or whoever the hell they are- continue speaking, but Andrea doesn't hear a word coming out of their mouths.

In a matter of moments, I can feel Andrea's whole demeanor change. The way she looks at the two individuals across from her sours.

Andrea is confused. How could they not tell her all this time? Why would they keep something like this from her?

*It makes her stomach turn.*

*"Is- is Alex my brother?"*

*Her parents are both silent for a moment.*

*"No," her mother whispers.*

*"Andrea, we're telling you this now because with the holidays coming up, your birth mother said she would like to see you so she doesn't have to spend another holiday alone."*

*"Fuck this," Andrea murmurs while wiping at her eyes with her sleeve.*

*Andrea stands up and walks to the door. She takes the car keys with her.*

*"Andrea, wait! Where are you going?" her mother calls after her.*

*"Shh. Let her go. She needs some time alone to process all of this," her father whispers to her mother.*

*Andrea bursts out the door into the blistering cold. As soon as she gets into the car, she pauses for a moment. Then she begins to bawl.*

*I cannot express the emotions she felt as she pulled out of the driveway.*

*Her entire world has just been pulled out from underneath her like a rug. She feels betrayed. She feels angry. She feels alone.*

*Andrea drives for a long time. Across town. Outside of town. She just keeps driving. She has to constantly wipe her eyes so she can see the road; her tears keep blurring her vision.*

*Andrea is unsure of what she should do. Where she should go. Andrea isn't sure of anything anymore.*

*Where will she spend the holidays? She will feel out of place wherever she goes. She couldn't go back to those people she had once called her family. They had betrayed her. They had lied to her. They were strangers to her.*

*And she most definitely won't go to her birth mother. She has no idea who she is or where she lives. She doesn't even know if she's Black or white.*

*And she doesn't want to see that bitch anyways.*

*What if she has another kid? She probably screwed them over too and ditched them.*

*Why did it take her so fucking long to want to see her own daughter?*

*Looks like that bitch will be spending another holiday alone.*

*Andrea is so fueled by anger, confusion, fear, and so many other conflicting emotions. She can't see an end in sight. Her entire life ahead of her seemed empty. Without love. Without family. And she just got rid of her one chance at having her own family.*

*I can't say I'm too surprised when Andrea decides to yank the wheel sideways.*

*The car skids and makes a terrible crash as it collides with the wall on the side of the road.*

*Andrea's eyes flit open. Bright lights flood her vision. She sees several figures looming over her. Strangers wearing masks. Doctors.*

*Her sense of hearing has come back to her and all she can hear is people shouting. A heart rate monitor beeps slowly. Andrea can feel herself being wheeled down the hallway.*

*She doesn't know who these people are. She feels as if she doesn't know who anyone is.*

*The entire world is comprised of strangers.*

*Andrea's head lolls to her side and she watches as the doorways rush past her. Room after room of people.*

*They stop moving her bed for a moment.*

*Andrea looks closely as the room she is stopped in front of.*

*There, within the room, several people stand around a bed weeping.*

*They are my parents and siblings.*

*And there, lying in the bed, is me.*

*Andrea overhears a bit of what the doctor is saying to my parents.*

*"Narcotics... alcohol... comatose..."*

119

*I want to scream and shout.*

*I try, but Andrea isn't saying anything.*

*My parents must've come looking for me when I didn't come home for the holidays and found my lifeless body hooked up to the IV. Dammit!*

*Then, over the sound of my own worrying, I distinctly hear Andrea's internal voice.*

*"It must be nice to have a real family."*

*As I peer into the room at my family crowding around my bed, the faintest smile creeps across her face.*

*I'm running out of time. I can feel it. Andrea is dying. I can feel her heart slowing.*

*Focusing her vision is becoming too difficult. Her mind is having difficulty grasping onto concrete thoughts. But there is one thing she's holding onto: Family.*

*The one thing she wants right now is to have someone she can call family.*

*She doesn't even feel the pain of the crash.*

*She only feels lonely.*

*I don't know what happens to me when she dies. The alcohol from Andrew and the drugs from Adam seeped through; what if death does too?*

*As much as I am hating my life and everything in it right now, death is not an option.*

*I don't want to admit it, but seeing my family around me has taken suicide out of the equation.*

*So, I guess it really boils down to two different options. Do I continue hopping from person to person, incessantly searching for a better life? Or do I return to my old body?*

*I can't do both.*

*After something like this, my parents would never let me out of their sight long enough for me to ride backseat in someone else.*

*The thought of that is slightly comforting. I know that my parents would stand watch over me forever because they would fear me getting harmed again.*

*And seeing the tears from their faces falling onto the bedsheets, their faces contorted in pain, the complete anguish, comforts me in a way.*

*This shows me that I would be missed.*

*My parents would miss me. My siblings would miss me. My family would miss me.*

*I can feel Andrea's body shutting down.*

*Her breathing slows.*

*Her heart beats to a slower rhythm.*

*Doctors yell somewhere in the background.*

*Andrea doesn't feel scared. She isn't in pain.*

*She just feels alone. So alone.*

*Andrea forces her eye open to catch one final glimpse into my room.*

*With her final ounce of strength, she smiles.*

*With a smile on her face, she closes her eyes for the last time.*

*And I open mine.*

**The beginning.**

# Acknowledgments:

A novel- while more of an individualistic artform as opposed to say, filmmaking, which is much more collaborative- takes a village to write.

I would like to extend my deepest appreciation to my editors, Mandi Summit and Shaina Clingempeel. Any mistakes are either intentional or can be attributed to the author. I would also like to extend my deepest thanks to the cover designer, Alejandro Martin, my liaison at Self-Publishing School, Barbara Hartzler, and the numerous beta-readers who wish to remain anonymous. Without all their contributions, this book would not be in your hands.

Finally, I would like to thank profusely: my fiancée, for always believing in me and all my zany endeavors, and the Benevolent Intelligent Being that created this beautiful, crazy universe.

Works Appropriated:

Dickens, Charles, and Harvey Dunn. A Tale of Two Cities. New York, Cosmopolitan Book Corporation, 1921

Melville, Herman, and Mead Schaeffer. Moby Dick. New York, Dodd, Mead, and Company, 1922